Barbie in A Mermaid Tale

By Mary Man-Kong
Based on the original screenplay by Elise Allen
Illustrated by Ulkutay Design Group and Pat Pakula

Special thanks to Vicki Jaeger, Monica Okazaki, Kathleen Warner, Emily Kelly, Christine Chang, Tanya Mann, Rob Hudnut, Tiffany J. Shuttleworth, Walter P. Martishius, Luke Carroll, Lil Reichmann, Pam Prostarr, David Lee, Anita Lee, Andrea Schimpl, Tulin Ulkutay, and Ayse Ulkutay

A Random House PICTUREBACK® Book
Random House 🏠 New York

BARBIE and associated trademarks and trade dress are owned by, and used under license from, Mattel, Inc.
Copyright © 2010 Mattel, Inc. All Rights Reserved.
Published in the United States by Random House Children's Books, a division of Random House, Inc.,
1745 Broadway, New York, NY 10019, and in Canada by Random House of Canada Limited, Toronto.
No part of this book may be reproduced or copied in any form without permission from the copyright owner.
Pictureback, Random House, and the Random House colophon are registered trademarks of Random House, Inc.
Library of Congress Control Number: 2009904823   ISBN: 978-0-375-85735-5
www.randomhouse.com/kids   Printed in the United States of America   20 19 18 17 16 15 14

Merliah Summers smiled as she rode the waves. Ever since she was a little girl, Merliah had been able to swim like a fish. Now she was one of the best surfers in Malibu.

As Merliah surfed, she thought everything was perfect—
until she noticed her hair. It was *turning bright pink!*

Shocked and embarrassed, Merliah wiped out and dove below the waves. To her amazement, she found that she could *breathe underwater!*

"Merliah?" someone said. A sparkly pink dolphin was talking to her! "My name is Zuma. I am a friend of your mother, Calissa. She is the mermaid queen of Oceana—but she needs your help."

Merliah couldn't believe that her mother was a magical mermaid—and that she was half mermaid herself! Merliah learned that when she was a baby, her mother's wicked sister, Eris, had taken over Oceana. The fortune-telling Destinies had foretold that Merliah would one day defeat Eris. So to protect her baby daughter, Calissa had sent Merliah to live with her human grandfather in Malibu.

Merliah just wanted her hair—and her life—back the way it was. *Maybe my mother's magic can help me return to normal,* Merliah thought. So she agreed to help.

With Zuma as her guide, Merliah journeyed underwater to the most gorgeous place she had ever seen! Oceana was bustling with colorful fish and fashionable merfolk.

"Amazing!" Merliah exclaimed.

"We'll have to disguise your legs," Zuma told Merliah.
She didn't want anyone to know that the young surfer was
in Oceana—especially not Eris.

Zuma quickly brought Merliah to the boutique run by
her friends Xylie and Kayla.

"Tail makeover!" Xylie and Kayla exclaimed.

At the palace, Eris snuck down to the secret dungeon where Calissa was locked away. The evil mermaid had learned that Merliah was in Oceana.

"Tell me where she is," Eris snarled at Calissa.

But Calissa refused to answer, to protect Merliah.

Meanwhile, the Destinies had told Merliah how to stop
Eris. She needed to complete three important tasks.

The first task was to find the Celestial Comb, hidden in
the Yafos Caves. No mermaid could climb the steep rock wall
to reach the comb. But Merliah had legs, and she scaled the
wall quickly. "I've got it!" she cried triumphantly.

The second task was to impress a dreamfish so that it would grant her a wish. Zuma knew exactly where the dreamfish could be found: in the Adenato Current. The powerful swirling water was impossible to swim in—but Merliah could surf it! The dreamfish were amazed.

"Call when you need me, and I will come," promised one young dreamfish.

The third task was the hardest. Merliah needed the necklace that Eris always wore around her neck. Merliah knew that Eris would appear at her daily festival, so she came up with a plan. Merliah, Xylie, and Kayla started singing to distract Eris.

"You're the queen of the waves!" sang the friends.

As Eris watched the show delightedly, Merliah snuck up behind her—and snatched the necklace!

"Stop her!" Eris cried.

The evil mermaid's manta sharks swam after Merliah and ripped off her fake tail!

"You!" Eris cried, realizing that Merliah was Calissa's daughter. Eris quickly captured the young surfer in a powerful whirlpool.

Merliah called for the dreamfish. He appeared and offered to return her to her normal life in Malibu. Merliah was tempted. But her mother and Oceana needed her, so she decided to stay and help.

Suddenly, Merliah's legs magically transformed into a sparkly *real* mermaid tail. Merliah couldn't believe it!

"I am Merliah, half-mermaid princess of Oceana," she cried proudly, and leapt out of the whirlpool. "And it is my duty to protect my subjects."

"Get her!" Eris ordered her guards.

"You don't need to listen to her," Merliah said. "I am the rightful heir to the throne. I have the Celestial Comb!"

Enraged, Eris tried to push Merliah back into the whirlpool. But Merliah quickly swam out of the way. The wicked mermaid was sucked into the powerful swirling water and transported to the deepest, darkest trench in the ocean.

The crowd cheered. Eris was gone forever!

Calissa was overjoyed to see her daughter. She wanted Merliah to stay in Oceana. Merliah was happy, too—but she missed her human life in Malibu. Calissa hugged Merliah and placed a magical necklace around her neck. Whenever she wished on the necklace, Merliah could transform from human to mermaid—and back again. "Then you can move easily between the human world and the underwater world," Calissa said.

Merliah was thrilled that she would have a home in both worlds!